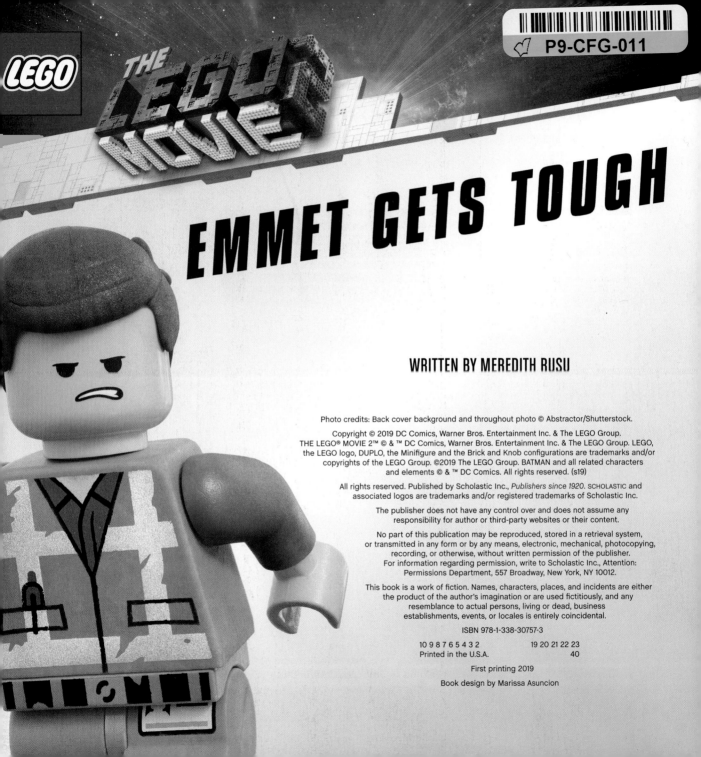

THE LEGO MOVIE

EMMET GETS TOUGH

WRITTEN BY MEREDITH RUSU

Copyright © 2019 DC Comics, Warner Bros. Entertainment Inc. & The LEGO Group.
THE LEGO® MOVIE 2™ © & ™ DC Comics, Warner Bros. Entertainment Inc. & The LEGO Group. LEGO, the LEGO logo, DUPLO, the Minifigure and the Brick and Knob configurations are trademarks and/or copyrights of the LEGO Group. ©2019 The LEGO Group. BATMAN and all related characters and elements © & ™ DC Comics. All rights reserved. (s19)

ISBN 978-1-338-30757-3

10 9 8 7 6 5 4 3 2   19 20 21 22 23
Printed in the U.S.A.   40

First printing 2019

Book design by Marissa Asuncion

Hi there! My name is Emmet. You might remember me as the guy who turned out to be The Special and saved everyone from Lord Business on Taco Tuesday. Boy, that sure was a long time ago! Back then, my friends and I thought everything in Bricksburg was going to be totally awesome forever and ever.

But . . . then we kind of got invaded by giant aliens called DUPLOs. They flew in on spaceships, ate all our bricks, and destroyed everything in sight. Now Bricksburg is called Apocalypseburg. It's a little less fun, to say the least.

Everyone here has gotten super tough and dusty. Even the coffee shop guy has a hard-core hairstyle and don't-mess-with-me face. But in spite of Apocalypseburg having an end-of-the-world vibe going on, I like to think that everything can *still* be awesome.

I mean, at least we still *have* a coffee shop. And I can still listen to sweet tunes as I walk to work. And best of all, I still have all my friends! They mean more to me than anything in the world. As long as we're together, I can't help but see the bright side.

9:07

EVERYTHING IS AWESOME

♪ Popsa Nova Remix

♪ Tween Dream Remix

♪ Electro Crunk Remix

Speaking of my friends, they look a little different now, too. Benny is rocking a robotic claw arm.

Metalbeard has added a few more cannons and sharp objects to his wardrobe.

Unikitty goes by the name Ultrakatty and sports a mega-angry look. So that's new.

And Batman is even *more* dark and brooding than before. I didn't know that was possible! I guess everyone is changing with the times.

My friend Lucy has changed the most of all. She doesn't look so different on the outside. But I can tell on the inside she's feeling pretty down. She likes to talk in a deep, serious voice. And she always seems sad, like she is thinking about the way Bricksburg used to be.

I missed seeing Lucy happy. I knew I had to figure out a way to turn her frown upside down. And then, one day, I had the perfect idea.

I picked a little plot of unspoiled brick dust in the middle of the apocalypse wasteland, and I built Lucy a house!

It had a living room, a kitchen, a meditation room (for me), a brooding room (for her), a trampoline room, and even a toaster room so we could make waffles any time of day.

"I thought we could rebuild the future together," I told Lucy. "Make everything awesome again."

But instead of being happy, Lucy seemed sadder than ever. "Emmet," she said, "you have to stop pretending everything is awesome. It isn't."

"The Bricksburg we used to know is gone," she told me. "We have to be tough and battle-ready. Both of us."

"Yeah, I get it," I said. "That's why I've cultivated a totally hard-edge side that's super tough and . . ."

Just then, I saw something incredible streak across the sky.

"Look! It's a shooting star!" I cried. "Make a wish!"

But Lucy's face grew worried. "That's not a shooting star. It's a spaceship. One we haven't seen before. We have to get Ultrakatty here right now for a recon mission!"

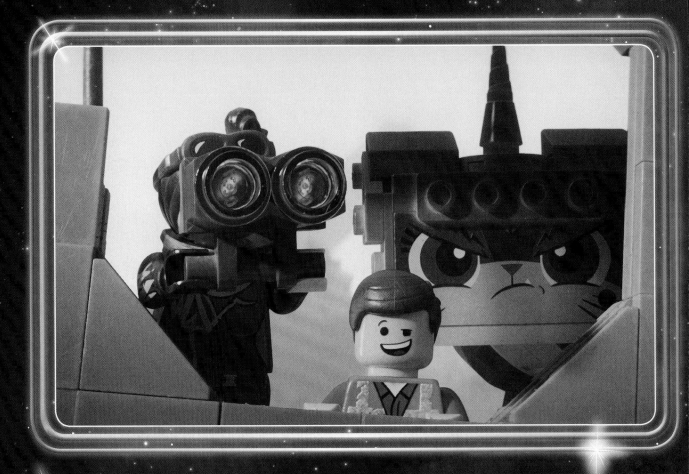

Soon, the three of us were in super-stealth mode. Like ninja spies but better. We watched the spaceship through Lucy's binoculars as it shined a bright pink laser beam on buildings, and pumped out catchy techno music.

"What is it *doing*?" Lucy asked.

"I don't know, but that beat is pretty fresh," I said. "Nntzz. Nntzz. Nntzz."

Suddenly, the spaceship turned and shined its bright pink laser on us.

Then, it started attacking! It shot pink, exploding, smiley-face hearts at us that were actually pretty cute until they burst into fiery flames.

We had to warn our friends about this new alien invader! So, we quick-built a tripped-out getaway car to escape.

"Super turbo engine!" said Lucy. "Check!"

"Super-safe taillight and blinker!" I said. "Check!"

The spaceship chased us through the ruined streets of Apocalypseburg. We dodged and ducked and dived, but it matched our every move. We just barely made it back to Batman's Citadel, where all our friends were, before the alien cornered us.

"I am General Mayhem," the alien said. "Intergalactic Naval Commander of the Systar System. Bring me your fiercest leader."

PERSONALITY ASSESSMENT
-WEAK
-NAIVE
-SIMPLE
-POWERLESS
-LESS THAN SPECIAL

"That would be me, obviously," said Batman.

But Lucy, Metalbeard, Benny, and Ultrakatty weren't so sure they agreed.

"Wait, guys," I said. "When everyone discovered we were all special on Taco Tuesday, didn't we all become leaders?"

The alien scanned me. "I sense no leadership qualities from you," it said.

"Hey, watch what you say about Emmet," Lucy stepped in. "He might be sweet and optimistic, and I know those aren't useful qualities anymore, and that he's not changing with the times, and in general isn't tough enough. But this guy is *The* Special."

"Not tough enough?" I whispered. *Did Lucy really think that about me?*

"Silence!" General Mayhem said. "I can't take everyone. I can fit maybe five."

"Take?" Lucy asked, worried.

"Your greatest leaders are cordially invited to a Ceremonial Ceremony at 5:15 p.m. tonight," the alien said.

With a blast of laser fire, the alien captured Batman, Ultrakatty, Metalbeard, Benny, and Lucy and trapped them in its spaceship! I tried to stop them from taking off, but I wasn't strong enough.

"Lucy!" I shouted. "No!"

"Emmet!" she cried. Then, in a bright flash, they were gone.

I couldn't believe it. Everyone I loved was in danger. And it was up to me to save them.

But if I was going to succeed, I would have to do something I'd never done before.

It was time to GET TOUGH. Let's DO it!